||| ||| ||| ||| ||| ||| ||| ||| ||| ||| |||
W9-CCP-105

A Visitor

The stranger came in—very dark and tall he looked in the firelight. He was carrying a box under his arm—a black, japanned box with little air holes in the lid. At the sight of the box, Jabez Stone gave a low cry and shrank into a corner of the room.

"Mr. Webster, I presume," said the stranger, very polite, but with his eyes glowing like a fox's deep in the woods.

"Attorney of record for Jabez Stone," said Dan'l Webster, but his eyes were glowing too. "Might I ask your name?"

"I've gone by a good many," said the stranger carelessly. "Perhaps Scratch will do for the evening. I'm often called that in these regions."

The Devil
and
Daniel Webster

AND OTHER STORIES

by STEPHEN VINCENT BENÉT

AN ARCHWAY PAPERBACK
POCKET BOOKS • NEW YORK

THE DEVIL AND DANIEL WEBSTER Copyright 1936, 1937 by Stephen Vincent Benét. Copyright © 1964, 1965 by Thomas C. Benét, Rachel B. Lewis and Stephanie Mahin. JOHNNY PYE AND THE FOOL-KILLER, copyright 1936, 1937 by Stephen Vincent Benét. Copyright © 1964, 1965, by Thomas C. Benét, Rachel B. Lewis and Stephanie Mahin. BY THE WATERS OF BABYLON copyright 1937 by Stephen Vincent Benét. Copyright © 1965, by Thomas C. Benét, Rachel B. Lewis and Stephen Benét Mahin.

POCKET BOOKS, a Simon & Schuster division of
GULF & WESTERN CORPORATION
1230 Avenue of the Americas, New York, N.Y. 10020

Copyright © 1967 by Simon and Schuster,
a division of Gulf & Western Corporation

Published by arrangement with Holt, Rinehart and Winston, Inc.

All rights reserved, including the right to reproduce
this book or portions thereof in any form whatsoever.
For information address Holt, Rinehart and Winston, Inc.
383 Madison Avenue, New York, N.Y. 10017

ISBN: 0-671-29943-3

First Pocket Books printing October, 1967

15   14   13   12   11   10   9   8   7

Trademarks registered in the United States and other countries.

Printed in the U.S.A.

CONTENTS

THE DEVIL
AND
DANIEL
WEBSTER

∼ ⁘ ∽

ILLUSTRATED BY *Harold Denison*

I

IT'S A STORY THEY TELL IN THE BORDER COUNTRY,
where Massachusetts joins Vermont and New
Hampshire.

Yes, Dan'l Webster's dead—or, at least, they
buried him. But every time there's a thunder-
storm around Marshfield, they say you can hear
his rolling voice in the hollows of the sky. And
they say that if you go to his grave and speak
loud and clear, "Dan'l Webster—Dan'l Webster!" the ground'll begin to shiver and the trees
begin to shake. And after a while you'll hear a
deep voice saying, "Neighbor, how stands the
Union?" Then you better answer the Union
stands as she stood, rock-bottomed and copper-
sheathed, one and indivisible, or he's liable to
rear right out of the ground. At least, that's
what I was told when I was a youngster.

You see, for a while, he was the biggest man

4

in the country. He never got to be President, but he was the biggest man. There were thousands that trusted in him right next to God Almighty, and they told stories about him and all the things that belonged to him that were like the stories of patriarchs and such. They said, when he stood up to speak, stars and stripes came right out in the sky, and once he spoke against a river and made it sink into the ground. They said, when he walked the woods with his fishing rod, Killall, the trout would jump out of the streams right into his pockets, for they knew it was no use putting up a fight against him; and, when he argued a case, he could turn on the harps of the blessed and the shaking of the earth underground. That was the kind of man he was, and his big farm up at Marshfield was suitable to him. The chickens he raised were all white meat down through the drumsticks, the cows were tended like children, and the big ram he called Goliath had horns with a curl like a morning-glory vine and could butt through an iron door. But Dan'l wasn't one of your gentlemen farmers; he knew all the ways of the land, and he'd be up by candlelight to see that the chores got done. A man with a mouth like a mastiff, a brow like a mountain and eyes like burning anthracite — that was Dan'l Webster in his prime. And the biggest case he argued never got written down in the books, for he argued it against the devil, nip and tuck and no holds barred. And this is the way I used to hear it told.

There was a man named Jabez Stone, lived at Cross Corners, New Hampshire. He wasn't a bad man to start with, but he was an unlucky man. If he planted corn, he got borers; if he planted potatoes, he got blight. He had good-enough land, but it didn't prosper him; he had a decent wife and children, but the more children he had, the less there was to feed them. If stones cropped up in his neighbor's field, boulders boiled up in his; if he had a horse with the spavins, he'd trade it for one with the staggers and give something extra. There's some folks bound to be like that, apparently. But one day Jabez Stone got sick of the whole business.

He'd been plowing that morning and he'd just broke the plowshare on a rock that he could have sworn hadn't been there yesterday. And, as he stood looking at the plowshare, the off horse began to cough—that ropy kind of cough that means sickness and horse doctors. There were two children down with the measles, his wife was ailing, and he had a whitlow on his thumb. It was about the last straw for Jabez Stone. "I vow," he said, and he looked around him kind of desperate—"I vow it's enough to make a man

6

want to sell his soul to the devil! And I would, too, for two cents!"

Then he felt a kind of queerness come over him at having said what he'd said; though, naturally, being a New Hampshireman, he wouldn't take it back. But, all the same, when it got to be evening and, as far as he could see, no notice had been taken, he felt relieved in his mind, for he was a religious man. But notice is always taken, sooner or later, just like the Good Book says. And, sure enough, next day, about suppertime, a soft-spoken, dark-dressed stranger drove up in a handsome buggy and asked for Jabez Stone.

Well, Jabez told his family it was a lawyer, come to see him about a legacy. But he knew who it was. He didn't like the looks of the stranger, nor the way he smiled with his teeth. They were white teeth, and plentiful—some say they were filed to a point, but I wouldn't vouch for that. And he didn't like it when the dog took one look at the stranger and ran away howling, with his tail between his legs. But having passed his word, more or less, he stuck to it, and they went out behind the barn and made their bargain. Jabez Stone had to prick his finger to sign, and the stranger lent him a silver pin. The wound healed clean, but it left a little white scar.

II

AFTER THAT, ALL OF A SUDDEN, THINGS BEGAN TO pick up and prosper for Jabez Stone. His cows got fat and his horses sleek, his crops were the envy of the neighborhood, and lightning might strike all over the valley, but it wouldn't strike his barn. Pretty soon, he was one of the prosperous people of the county; they asked him to stand for selectman, and he stood for it; there began to be talk of running him for state senate. All in all, you might say the Stone family was as happy and contented as cats in a dairy. And so they were, except for Jabez Stone.

He'd been contented enough, the first few years. It's a great thing when bad luck turns; it drives most other things out of your head. True, every now and then, especially in rainy weather, the little white scar on his finger would give him a twinge. And once a year, punctual as clockwork, the stranger with the handsome buggy would come driving by. But the sixth year, the stranger lighted, and, after that, his peace was over for Jabez Stone.

The stranger came up through the lower field, switching his boots with a cane—they were handsome black boots, but Jabez Stone never liked the look of them, particularly the toes. And, after he'd passed the time of day, he said, "Well, Mr. Stone, you're a hummer! It's a very pretty property you've got here, Mr. Stone."

"Well, some might favor it and others might not," said Jabez Stone, for he was a New Hampshireman.

"Oh, no need to decry your industry!" said the stranger, very easy, showing his teeth in a smile. "After all, we know what's been done, and it's been according to contract and specifications. So when—ahem—the mortgage falls due next year, you shouldn't have any regrets."

"Speaking of that mortgage, mister," said Jabez Stone, and he looked around for help to the earth and the sky, "I'm beginning to have one or two doubts about it."

"Doubts?" said the stranger, not quite so pleasantly.

"Why, yes," said Jabez Stone. "This being the U. S. A. and me always having been a

11

religious man." He cleared his throat and got bolder. "Yes, sir," he said, "I'm beginning to have considerable doubts as to that mortgage holding in court."

"There's courts and courts," said the stranger, clicking his teeth. "Still, we might as well have a look at the original document." And he hauled out a big black pocketbook, full of papers. "Sherwin, Slater, Stevens, Stone," he muttered. "I, Jabez Stone, for a term of seven years—Oh, it's quite in order, I think."

But Jabez Stone wasn't listening, for he saw something else flutter out of the black pocketbook. It was something that looked like a moth, but it wasn't a moth. And as Jabez Stone stared at it, it seemed to speak to him in a small sort of piping voice, terrible small and thin, but terrible human.

"Neighbor Stone!" it squeaked. "Neighbor Stone! Help me! For God's sake, help me!"

But before Jabez Stone could stir hand or foot, the stranger whipped out a big bandanna handkerchief, caught the creature in it, just like a butterfly, and started tying up the ends of the bandanna.

"Sorry for the interruption," he said. "As I was saying—"

But Jabez Stone was shaking all over like a scared horse.

"That's Miser Stevens' voice!" he said, in a croak. "And you've got him in your handkerchief!"

The stranger looked a little embarrassed.

"Yes, I really should have transferred him to the collecting box," he said with a simper, "but there were some rather unusual specimens there and I didn't want them crowded. Well, well, these little contretemps will occur."

"I don't know what you mean by contertan," said Jabez Stone, "but that was Miser Stevens' voice! And he ain't dead! You can't tell me he is! He was just as spry and mean as a woodchuck, Tuesday!"

"In the midst of life—" said the stranger, kind of pious. "Listen!" Then a bell began to toll in the valley and Jabez Stone listened, with the sweat running down his face. For he knew it was tolled for Miser Stevens and that he was dead.

"These long-standing accounts," said the stranger with a sigh; "one really hates to close them. But business is business."

He still had the bandanna in his hand, and Jabez Stone felt sick as he saw the cloth struggle and flutter.

"Are they all as small as that?" he asked hoarsely.

"Small?" said the stranger. "Oh, I see what

you mean. Why, they vary." He measured Jabez Stone with his eyes, and his teeth showed. "Don't worry, Mr. Stone," he said. "You'll go with a very good grade. I wouldn't trust you outside the collecting box. Now, a man like Dan'l Webster, of course—well, we'd have to build a special box for him, and even at that, I imagine the wing spread would astonish you. He'd certainly be a prize. I wish we could see our way clear to him. But, in your case, as I was saying—"

"Put that handkerchief away!" said Jabez Stone, and he began to beg and to pray. But the best he could get at the end was a three years' extension, with conditions.

But till you make a bargain like that, you've got no idea of how fast four years can run. By the last months of those years, Jabez Stone's known all over the state and there's talk of running him for governor—and it's dust and ashes in his mouth. For every day, when he gets up, he thinks, "There's one more night gone," and every night when he lies down, he thinks of the black pocketbook and the soul of Miser Stevens, and it makes him sick at heart. Till, finally, he can't bear it any longer, and, in the last days of the last year, he hitches up his horse and drives off to seek Dan'l Webster. For

Dan'l was born in New Hampshire, only a few miles from Cross Corners, and it's well known that he has a particular soft spot for old neighbors.

III

IT WAS EARLY IN THE MORNING WHEN HE GOT TO
Marshfield, but Dan'l was up already, talking
Latin to the farm hands and wrestling with the
ram, Goliath, and trying out a new trotter and
working up speeches to make against John C.
Calhoun. But when he heard a New Hampshireman had come to see him, he dropped
everything else he was doing, for that was
Dan'l's way. He gave Jabez Stone a breakfast
that five men couldn't eat, went into the living
history of every man and woman in Cross
Corners, and finally asked him how he could
serve him.

Jabez Stone allowed that it was a kind of
mortgage case.

"Well, I haven't pleaded a mortgage case in
a long time, and I don't generally plead now,

except before the Supreme Court," said Dan'l, "but if I can, I'll help you."

"Then I've got hope for the first time in ten years," said Jabez Stone, and told him the details.

Dan'l walked up and down as he listened, hands behind his back, now and then asking a question, now and then plunging his eyes at the floor, as if they'd bore through it like gimlets. When Jabez Stone had finished, Dan'l puffed out his cheeks and blew. Then he turned to Jabez Stone and a smile broke over his face like the sunrise over Monadnock.

"You've certainly given yourself the devil's own row to hoe, Neighbor Stone," he said, "but I'll take your case."

"You'll take it?" said Jabez Stone, hardly daring to believe.

"Yes," said Dan'l Webster. "I've got about seventy-five other things to do and the Missouri Compromise to straighten out, but I'll take your case. For if two New Hampshiremen aren't a match for the devil, we might as well give the country back to the Indians."

Then he shook Jabez Stone by the hand and said, "Did you come down here in a hurry?"

"Well, I admit I made time," said Jabez Stone.

"You'll go back faster," said Dan'l Webster,

and he told 'em to hitch up Constitution and Constellation to the carriage. They were matched grays with one white forefoot, and they stepped like greased lightning.

Well, I won't describe how excited and pleased the whole Stone family was to have the great Dan'l Webster for a guest, when they finally got there. Jabez Stone had lost his hat on the way, blown off when they overtook a wind, but he didn't take much account of that. But after supper he sent the family off to bed, for he had most particular business with Mr. Webster. Mrs. Stone wanted them to sit in the front parlor, but Dan'l Webster knew front parlors and said he preferred the kitchen. So it was there they sat, waiting for the stranger, with a jug on the table between them and a bright fire on the hearth—the stranger being scheduled to show up on the stroke of midnight, according to specification.

Well, most men wouldn't have asked for better company than Dan'l Webster and a jug. But with every tick of the clock Jabez Stone got sadder and sadder. His eyes roved round, and though he sampled the jug you could see he couldn't taste it. Finally, on the stroke of 11:30, he reached over and grabbed Dan'l Webster by the arm.

"Mr. Webster, Mr. Webster!" he said, and

his voice was shaking with fear and a desperate courage. "For God's sake, Mr. Webster, harness your horses and get away from this place while you can!"

"You've brought me a long way, neighbor, to tell me you don't like my company," said Dan'l Webster, quite peaceable, pulling at the jug.

"Miserable wretch that I am!" groaned Jabez Stone. "I've brought you a devilish way, and now I see my folly. Let him take me if he wills. I don't hanker after it, I must say, but I can stand it. But you're the Union's stay and New Hampshire's pride! He mustn't get you, Mr. Webster! He mustn't get you!"

Dan'l Webster looked at the distracted man, all gray and shaking in the firelight, and laid a hand on his shoulder.

"I'm obliged to you, Neighbor Stone," he said gently. "It's kindly thought of. But there's a jug on the table and a case in hand. And I never left a jug or a case half finished in my life."

And just at that moment there was a sharp rap on the door.

"Ah," said Dan'l Webster, very coolly, "I thought your clock was a trifle slow, Neighbor Stone." He stepped to the door and opened it. "Come in!" he said.

The stranger came in—very dark and tall he

looked in the firelight. He was carrying a box under his arm—a black, japanned box with little air holes in the lid. At the sight of the box, Jabez Stone gave a low cry and shrank into a corner of the room.

"Mr. Webster, I presume," said the stranger, very polite, but with his eyes glowing like a fox's deep in the woods.

"Attorney of record for Jabez Stone," said Dan'l Webster, but his eyes were glowing too. "Might I ask your name?"

"I've gone by a good many," said the stranger carelessly. "Perhaps Scratch will do for the evening. I'm often called that in these regions."

Then he sat down at the table and poured himself a drink from the jug. The liquor was cold in the jug, but it came steaming into the glass.

"And now," said the stranger, smiling and showing his teeth, "I shall call upon you, as a law-abiding citizen, to assist me in taking possession of my property."

Well, with that the argument began—and it went hot and heavy. At first, Jabez Stone had a flicker of hope, but when he saw Dan'l Webster being forced back at point after point, he just sat scrunched in his corner, with his eyes on that japanned box. For there wasn't any doubt as to the deed or the signature—that was the worst of it. Dan'l Webster twisted and turned and thumped his fist on the table, but he couldn't get away from that. He offered to compromise the case; the stranger wouldn't hear of it. He pointed out the property had increased in value, and state senators ought to be worth more; the stranger stuck to the letter of the law. He was a great lawyer, Dan'l Webster, but we know who's the King of Lawyers, as the Good Book tells us, and it seemed as if, for the first time, Dan'l Webster had met his match.

Finally, the stranger yawned a little. "Your spirited efforts on behalf of your client do you credit, Mr. Webster," he said, "but if you have no more arguments to adduce, I'm rather pressed for time—" and Jabez Stone shuddered.

Dan'l Webster's brow looked dark as a thundercloud. "Pressed or not, you shall not have this man!" he thundered. "Mr. Stone is an American citizen, and no American citizen may be forced into the service of a foreign prince. We fought England for that in '12 and we'll fight all hell for it again!"

"Foreign?" said the stranger. "And who calls me a foreigner?"

"Well, I never yet heard of the dev—of your claiming American citizenship," said Dan'l Webster with surprise.

"And who with better right?" said the stranger, with one of his terrible smiles. "When the first wrong was done to the first Indian, I was there. When the first slaver put out for the Congo, I stood on her deck. Am I not in your books and stories and beliefs, from the first settlements on? Am I not spoken of, still, in every church in New England? 'Tis true the North claims me for a Southerner, and the South for a Northerner, but I am neither. I am merely an honest American like yourself—and of the best descent—for, to tell the truth, Mr. Webster, though I don't like to boast of it, my name is older in this country than yours."

"Aha!" said Dan'l Webster, with the veins standing out in his forehead. "Then I stand on the Constitution! I demand a trial for my client!"

"The case is hardly one for an ordinary court," said the stranger, his eyes flickering. "And, indeed, the lateness of the hour—"

"Let it be any court you choose, so it is an American judge and an American jury!" said Dan'l Webster in his pride. "Let it be the quick or the dead; I'll abide the issue!"

"You have said it," said the stranger, and pointed his finger at the door. And with that, and all of a sudden, there was a rushing of wind outside and a noise of footsteps. They came, clear and distinct, through the night. And yet, they were not like the footsteps of living men.

"In God's name, who comes by so late?" cried Jabez Stone, in an ague of fear.

"The jury Mr. Webster demands," said the stranger, sipping at his boiling glass. "You must pardon the rough appearance of one or two; they will have come a long way."

IV

AND WITH THAT THE FIRE BURNED BLUE AND THE
door blew open and twelve men entered, one
by one.

If Jabez Stone had been sick with terror before, he was blind with terror now. For there
was Walter Butler, the loyalist, who spread fire
and horror through the Mohawk Valley in the
times of the Revolution; and there was Simon
Girty, the renegade, who saw white men burned
at the stake and whooped with the Indians to
see them burn. His eyes were green, like a
catamount's, and the stains on his hunting shirt
did not come from the blood of the deer. King
Philip was there, wild and proud as he had
been in life, with the great gash in his head
that gave him his death wound, and cruel
Governor Dale, who broke men on the wheel.
There was Morton of Merry Mount, who so

vexed the Plymouth Colony, with his flushed, loose, handsome face and his hate of the godly. There was Teach, the bloody pirate, with his black beard curling on his breast. The Reverend John Smeet, with his strangler's hands and his Geneva gown, walked as daintily as he had to the gallows. The red print of the rope was still around his neck, but he carried a perfumed handkerchief in one hand. One and all, they came into the room with the fires of hell still upon them, and the stranger named their names and their deeds as they came, till the tale of twelve was told. Yet the stranger had told the truth—they had all played a part in America.

"Are you satisfied with the jury, Mr. Webster?" said the stranger mockingly, when they had taken their places.

The sweat stood upon Dan'l Webster's brow, but his voice was clear.

"Quite satisfied," he said. "Though I miss General Arnold from the company."

"Benedict Arnold is engaged upon other business," said the stranger, with a glower. "Ah, you asked for a justice, I believe."

He pointed his finger once more, and a tall man, soberly clad in Puritan garb, with the burning gaze of the fanatic, stalked into the room and took his judge's place.

"Justice Hathorne is a jurist of experience,"

said the stranger. "He presided at certain witch trials once held in Salem. There were others who repented of the business later, but not he."

"Repent of such notable wonders and undertakings?" said the stern old justice. "Nay, hang them—hang them all!" And he muttered to himself in a way that struck ice into the soul of Jabez Stone.

Then the trial began, and, as you might expect, it didn't look anyways good for the defense. And Jabez Stone didn't make much of a witness in his own behalf. He took one look at Simon Girty and screeched, and they had to put him back in his corner in a kind of swoon.

It didn't halt the trial, though; the trial went on, as trials do. Dan'l Webster had faced some hard juries and hanging judges in his time, but this was the hardest he'd ever faced, and he knew it. They sat there with a kind of glitter in their eyes, and the stranger's smooth voice went on and on. Every time he'd raise an objection, it'd be "Objection sustained," but whenever Dan'l objected, it'd be "Objection denied." Well, you couldn't expect fair play from a fellow like this Mr. Scratch.

It got to Dan'l in the end, and he began to heat, like iron in the forge. When he got up to speak he was going to flay that stranger with every trick known to the law, and the judge and jury too. He didn't care if it was contempt of court or what would happen to him for it. He didn't care any more what happened to Jabez Stone. He just got madder and madder, thinking of what he'd say. And yet, curiously enough, the more he thought about it, the less he was able to arrange his speech in his mind.

Till, finally, it was time for him to get up on his feet, and he did so, all ready to bust out with lightnings and denunciations. But before he started he looked over the judge and jury for a moment, such being his custom. And he noticed the glitter in their eyes was twice as strong as before, and they all leaned forward. Like hounds just before they get the fox, they looked, and the blue mist of evil in the room thickened as he watched them. Then he saw what he'd been about to do, and he wiped his forehead, as a man might who's just escaped falling into a pit in the dark.

For it was him they'd come for, not only Jabez Stone. He read it in the glitter of their eyes and in the way the stranger hid his mouth with one hand. And if he fought them with their own weapons, he'd fall into their power; he knew that, though he couldn't have told you how. It was his own anger and horror that burned in their eyes; and he'd have to wipe that out or the case was lost. He stood there for a moment, his black eyes burning like anthracite. And then he began to speak.

He started off in a low voice, though you could hear every word. They say he could call on the harps of the blessed when he chose. And this was just as simple and easy as a man could talk. But he didn't start out by condemning or reviling. He was talking about the things that make a country a country, and a man a man.

And he began with the simple things that everybody's known and felt—the freshness of a fine morning when you're young, and the taste of food when you're hungry, and the new day that's every day when you're a child. He took them up and he turned them in his hands. They were good things for any man. But without freedom, they sickened. And when he talked of those enslaved, and the sorrows of slavery, his voice got like a big bell. He talked of the early days of America and the men who had made those days. It wasn't a spread-eagle speech, but he made you see it. He admitted all the wrong that had ever been done. But he showed how, out of the wrong and the right, the suffering and the starvations, something new had come. And everybody had played a part in it, even the traitors.

Then he turned to Jabez Stone and showed him as he was—an ordinary man who'd had hard luck and wanted to change it. And, because he'd wanted to change it, now he was going to be punished for all eternity. And yet there was good in Jabez Stone, and he showed that good. He was hard and mean, in some ways, but he was a man. There was sadness in being a man, but it was a proud thing too. And he showed what the pride of it was till you couldn't help feeling it. Yes, even in hell, if a man was a man, you'd know it. And he wasn't pleading for any one person any more, though his voice rang like an organ. He was telling the story and the failures and the endless journey of mankind. They got tricked and trapped and bamboozled, but it was a great journey. And no demon that was ever foaled could know the inwardness of it—it took a man to do that.

V

THE FIRE BEGAN TO DIE ON THE HEARTH AND
the wind before morning to blow. The light
was getting gray in the room when Dan'l Webster finished. And his words came back at the
end to New Hampshire ground, and the one
spot of land that each man loves and clings to.
He painted a picture of that, and to each one
of that jury he spoke of things long forgotten.
For his voice could search the heart, and that
was his gift and his strength. And to one, his
voice was like the forest and its secrecy, and to
another like the sea and the storms of the sea;
and one heard thè cry of his lost nation in it,
and another saw a little harmless scene he
hadn't remembered for years. But each saw
something. And when Dan'l Webster finished
he didn't know whether or not he'd saved Jabez

Stone. But he knew he'd done a miracle. For the glitter was gone from the eyes of judge and jury, and, for the moment, they were men again, and knew they were men.

"The defense rests," said Dan'l Webster, and stood there like a mountain. His ears were still ringing with his speech, and he didn't hear anything else till he heard Judge Hathorne say, "The jury will retire to consider its verdict."

Walter Butler rose in his place and his face had a dark, gay pride on it.

"The jury has considered its verdict," he said, and looked the stranger full in the eye. "We find for the defendant, Jabez Stone."

With that, the smile left the stranger's face, but Walter Butler did not flinch.

"Perhaps 'tis not strictly in accordance with the evidence," he said, "but even the damned may salute the eloquence of Mr. Webster."

With that, the long crow of a rooster split the gray morning sky, and judge and jury were gone from the room like a puff of smoke and as if they had never been there. The stranger turned to Dan'l Webster, smiling wryly. "Major Butler was always a bold man," he said. "I had not thought him quite so bold. Nevertheless, my congratulations, as between two gentlemen."

"I'll have that paper first, if you please," said

Dan'l Webster, and he took it and tore it into
four pieces. It was queerly warm to the touch.
"And now," he said, "I'll have you!" and his
hand came down like a bear trap on the
stranger's arm. For he knew that once you
bested anybody like Mr. Scratch in fair fight,
his power on you was gone. And he could see
that Mr. Scratch knew it too.

The stranger twisted and wriggled, but he
couldn't get out of that grip. "Come, come, Mr.
Webster," he said, smiling palely. "This sort of
thing is ridic—ouch!—is ridiculous. If you're
worried about the costs of the case, naturally,
I'd be glad to pay—"

"And so you shall!" said Dan'l Webster, shaking him till his teeth rattled. "For you'll sit
right down at that table and draw up a document, promising never to bother Jabez Stone
nor his heirs or assigns nor any other New
Hampshireman till doomsday! For any hades
we want to raise in this state, we can raise our-
selves, without assistance from strangers."

"Ouch!" said the stranger. "Ouch! Well, they
never did run very big to the barrel, but—ouch!
—I agree!"

So he sat down and drew up the document.
But Dan'l Webster kept his hand on his coat
collar all the time.

"And, now, may I go?" said the stranger,

quite humble, when Dan'l'd seen the document was in proper and legal form.

"Go?" said Dan'l, giving him another shake. "I'm still trying to figure out what I'll do with you. For you've settled the costs of the case, but you haven't settled with me. I think I'll take you back to Marshfield," he said, kind of reflective. "I've got a ram there named Goliath that can butt through an iron door. I'd kind of like to turn you loose in his field and see what he'd do."

Well, with that the stranger began to beg and to plead. And he begged and he pled so humble that finally Dan'l, who was naturally kindhearted, agreed to let him go. The stranger seemed terrible grateful for that and said, just to show they were friends, he'd tell Dan'l's fortune before leaving. So Dan'l agreed to that, though he didn't take much stock in fortune-tellers ordinarily.

But, naturally, the stranger was a little different. Well, he pried and he peered at the lines in Dan'l's hands. And he told him one thing and another that was quite remarkable. But they were all in the past.

"Yes, all that's true, and it happened," said Dan'l Webster. "But what's to come in the future?"

The stranger grinned, kind of happily, and

shook his head. "The future's not as you think it," he said. "It's dark. You have a great ambition, Mr. Webster."

"I have," said Dan'l firmly, for everybody knew he wanted to be President.

"It seems almost within your grasp," said the stranger, "but you will not attain it. Lesser men will be made President and you will be passed over."

"And, if I am, I'll still be Daniel Webster," said Dan'l. "Say on."

"You have two strong sons," said the stranger, shaking his head. "You look to found a line. But each will die in war and neither reach greatness."

"Live or die, they are still my sons," said Dan'l Webster. "Say on."

"You have made great speeches," said the stranger. "You will make more."

"Ah," said Dan'l Webster.

"But the last great speech you make will turn many of your own against you," said the stranger. "They will call you Ichabod; they will call you by other names. Even in New England some will say you have turned your coat and sold your country, and their voices will be loud against you till you die."

"So it is an honest speech, it does not matter

what men say," said Dan'l Webster. Then he looked at the stranger and their glances locked.

"One question," he said. "I have fought for the Union all my life. Will I see that fight won against those who would tear it apart?"

"Not while you live," said the stranger, grimly, "but it will be won. And after you are dead, there are thousands who will fight for your cause, because of words that you spoke."

"Why, then, you long-barreled, slab-sided, lantern-jawed, fortune-telling note shaver!" said Dan'l Webster, with a great roar of laughter, "be off with you to your own place before I put my mark on you! For, by the thirteen original colonies, I'd go to the Pit itself to save the Union!"

And with that he drew back his foot for a kick that would have stunned a horse. It was only the tip of his shoe that caught the stranger, but he went flying out of the door with his collecting box under his arm.

"And now," said Dan'l Webster, seeing Jabez Stone beginning to rouse from his swoon, "let's see what's left in the jug, for it's dry work talking all night. I hope there's pie for breakfast, Neighbor Stone."

But they say that whenever the devil comes near Marshfield, even now, he gives it a wide berth. And he hasn't been seen in the state of New Hampshire from that day to this. I'm not talking about Massachusetts or Vermont.

BY THE WATERS
OF BABYLON

THE NORTH AND THE WEST AND THE SOUTH ARE good hunting ground, but it is forbidden to go east. It is forbidden to go to any of the Dead Places except to search for metal and then he who touches the metal must be a priest or the son of a priest. Afterwards, both the man and the metal must be purified. These are the rules and the laws; they are well made. It is forbidden to cross the great river and look upon the place that was the Place of the Gods—this is most strictly forbidden. We do not even say its name though we know its name. It is there that spirits live, and demons—it is there that there are the ashes of the Great Burning. These things are forbidden—they have been forbidden since the beginning of time.

My father is a priest; I am the son of a priest. I have been in the Dead Places near us, with my father—at first, I was afraid. When my father went into the house to search for the metal, I stood by the door and my heart felt small and weak. It was a dead man's house, a spirit house. It did not have the smell of man, though there were old bones in a corner. But it is not fitting that a priest's son should show fear. I looked at the bones in the shadow and kept my voice still.

Then my father came out with the metal—a good, strong piece. He looked at me with both eyes but I had not run away. He gave me the metal to hold—I took it and did not die. So he knew that I was truly his son and would be a priest in my time. That was when I was very young—nevertheless, my brothers would not have done it, though they are good hunters. After that, they gave me the good piece of meat and the warm corner by the fire. My father watched over me—he was glad that I should be a priest. But when I boasted or wept without a reason, he punished me more strictly than my brothers. That was right.

After a time, I myself was allowed to go into the dead houses and search for metal. So I learned the ways of those houses—and if I saw bones, I was no longer afraid. The bones are light and old—sometimes they will fall into dust if you touch them. But that is a great sin.

I was taught the chants and the spells—I was taught how to stop the running of blood from a wound and many secrets. A priest must know many secrets—that was what my father said. If the hunters think we do all things by chants and spells, they may believe so—it does not hurt them. I was taught how to read in the old books and how to make the old writings—that was hard and took a long time. My knowledge made me happy—it was like a fire in my heart. Most of all, I liked to hear of the Old Days and the stories of the gods. I asked myself many questions that I could not answer, but it was good to ask them. At night, I would lie awake and listen to the wind—it seemed to me that it was the voice of the gods as they flew through the air.

We are not ignorant like the Forest People—our women spin wool on the wheel, our priests wear white robes. We do not eat grubs from the tree, we have not forgotten the old writings, although they are hard to understand. Nevertheless, my knowledge and my lack of knowledge burned in me—I wished to know more. When I was a man at last, I came to my father and said, "It is time for me to go on my journey. Give me your leave."

He looked at me for a long time, stroking his beard, then he said at last, "Yes. It is time."

That night, in the house of the priesthood, I asked for and received purification. My body hurt but my spirit was a cool stone. It was my father himself who questioned me about my dreams.

He bade me look into the smoke of the fire and see—I saw and told what I saw. It was what I have always seen—a river and, beyond it, a great Dead Place and in it the gods walking. I have always thought about that. His eyes were stern when I told him—he was no longer my father but a priest. He said, "This is a strong dream."

"It is mine," I said, while the smoke waved and my head felt light. They were singing the Star song in the outer chamber and it was like the buzzing of bees in my head.

He asked me how the gods were dressed and I told him how they were dressed. We know how they were dressed from the book, but I saw them as if they were before me. When I had finished, he threw the sticks three times and studied them as they fell.

"This is a very strong dream," he said. "It may eat you up."

"I am not afraid," I said and looked at him with both eyes. My voice sounded thin in my ears but that was because of the smoke.

He touched me on the breast and the forehead. He gave me the bow and the three arrows.

"Take them," he said. "It is forbidden to travel east. It is forbidden to cross the river. It is forbidden to go to the Place of the Gods. All these things are forbidden."

"All these things are forbidden," I said, but it was my voice that spoke and not my spirit. He looked at me again.

"My son," he said. "Once I had young dreams. If your dreams do not eat you up, you may be a great priest. If they eat you, you are still my son. Now go on your journey."

I went fasting, as is the law. My body hurt but not my heart. When the dawn came, I was out of sight of the village. I prayed and purified myself, waiting for a sign. The sign was an eagle. It flew east.

Sometimes signs are sent by bad spirits. I waited again on the flat rock, fasting, taking no food. I was very still—I could feel the sky above me and the earth beneath. I waited till the sun was beginning to sink. Then three deer passed in the valley, going east—they did not wind me or see me. There was a white fawn with them— a very great sign.

I followed them, at a distance, waiting for what would happen. My heart was troubled about going east, yet I knew that I must go.

My head hummed with my fasting—I did not even see the panther spring upon the white fawn. But, before I knew it, the bow was in my hand. I shouted and the panther lifted his head from the fawn. It is not easy to kill a panther with one arrow but the arrow went through his eye and into his brain. He died as he tried to spring—he rolled over, tearing at the ground. Then I knew I was meant to go east—I knew that was my journey. When the night came, I made my fire and roasted meat.

It is eight suns' journey to the east and a man passes by many Dead Places. The Forest People are afraid of them but I am not. Once I made my fire on the edge of a Dead Place at night and, next morning, in the dead house, I found a good knife, little rusted. That was small to what came afterward but it made my heart feel big. Always when I looked for game, it was in front of my arrow, and twice I passed hunting parties of the Forest People without their knowing. So I knew my magic was strong and my journey clean, in spite of the law.

Toward the setting of the eighth sun, I came to the banks of the great river. It was half-a-day's journey after I had left the god-road—we do not use the god-roads now for they are falling apart into great blocks of stone, and the

forest is safer going. A long way off, I had seen
the water through trees but the trees were thick.
At last, I came out upon an open place at the
top of a cliff. There was the great river below,
like a giant in the sun. It is very long, very
wide. It could eat all the streams we know and
still be thirsty. Its name is Ou-dis-sun, the
Sacred, the Long. No man of my tribe had seen
it, not even my father, the priest. It was magic
and I prayed.

Then I raised my eyes and looked south. It
was there, the Place of the Gods.

How can I tell what it was like—you do not
know. It was there, in the red light, and they
were too big to be houses. It was there with the
red light upon it, mighty and ruined. I knew
that in another moment the gods would see me.
I covered my eyes with my hands and crept
back into the forest.

Surely, that was enough to do, and live. Surely it was enough to spend the night upon the
cliff. The Forest People themselves do not come
near. Yet, all through the night, I knew that I
should have to cross the river and walk in the
places of the gods, although the gods ate me
up. My magic did not help me at all and yet
there was a fire in my bowels, a fire in my
mind. When the sun rose, I thought, "My

journey has been clean. Now I will go home from my journey." But, even as I thought so, I knew I could not. If I went to the Place of the Gods, I would surely die, but, if I did not go, I could never be at peace with my spirit again. It is better to lose one's life than one's spirit, if one is a priest and the son of a priest.

Nevertheless, as I made the raft, the tears ran out of my eyes. The Forest People could have killed me without fight, if they had come upon me then, but they did not come. When the raft was made, I said the sayings for the dead and painted myself for death. My heart was cold as a frog and my knees like water, but the burning in my mind would not let me have peace. As I pushed the raft from the shore, I began my death song—I had the right. It was a fine song.

"I am John, son of John," I sang. "My people are the Hill People. They are the men.
I go into the Dead Places but I am not slain.
I take the metal from the Dead Places but I am not blasted.
I travel upon the god-roads and am not afraid. E-yah! I have killed the panther, I have killed the fawn!
E-yah! I have come to the great river. No man has come there before.

It is forbidden to go east, but I have gone, forbidden to go on the great river, but I am
there.

Open your hearts, you spirits, and hear my
song.

Now I go to the Place of the Gods, I shall not
return.

My body is painted for death and my limbs
weak, but my heart is big as I go to the
Place of the Gods!"

All the same, when I came to the Place of the
Gods, I was afraid, afraid. The current of the
great river is very strong—it gripped my raft
with its hands. That was magic, for the river
itself is wide and calm. I could feel evil spirits
about me, in the bright morning; I could feel
their breath on my neck as I was swept down
the stream. Never have I been so much alone—
I tried to think of my knowledge, but it was a
squirrel's heap of winter nuts. There was no
strength in my knowledge any more and I felt
small and naked as a new-hatched bird—alone
upon the great river, the servant of the gods.

Yet, after a while, my eyes were opened and
I saw. I saw both banks of the river—I saw that
once there had been god-roads across it, though
now they were broken and fallen like broken
vines. Very great they were, and wonderful and

ᴐroken—broken in the time of the Great Burning when the fire fell out of the sky. And always the current took me nearer to the Place of the Gods, and the huge ruins rose before my eyes.

I do not know the customs of rivers—we are the People of the Hills. I tried to guide my raft with the pole but it spun around. I thought the river meant to take me past the Place of the Gods and out into the Bitter Water of the legends. I grew angry then—my heart felt strong. I said aloud, "I am a priest and the son of a priest!" The gods heard me—they showed me how to paddle with the pole on one side of the raft. The current changed itself—I drew near to the Place of the Gods.

When I was very near, my raft struck and turned over. I can swim in our lakes—I swam to the shore. There was a great spike of rusted metal sticking out into the river—I hauled myself up upon it and sat there, panting. I had saved my bow and two arrows and the knife I found in the Dead Place but that was all. My raft went whirling downstream toward the Bitter Water. I looked after it, and thought if it had trod me under, at least I would be safely dead. Nevertheless, when I had dried my bow-string and re-strung it, I walked forward to the Place of the Gods.

It felt like ground underfoot; it did not burn

me. It is not true what some of the tales say, that the ground there burns forever, for I have been there. Here and there were the marks and stains of the Great Burning, on the ruins, that is true. But they were old marks and old stains. It is not true either, what some of our priests say, that it is an island covered with fogs and enchantments. It is not. It is a great Dead Place—greater than any Dead Place we know. Everywhere in it there are god-roads, though most are cracked and broken. Everywhere there are the ruins of the high towers of the gods.

How shall I tell what I saw? I went carefully, my strung bow in my hand, my skin ready for danger. There should have been the wailings of spirits and the shrieks of demons, but there were not. It was very silent and sunny where I had landed—the wind and the rain and the birds that drop seeds had done their work—the grass grew in the cracks of the broken stone. It is a fair island—no wonder the gods built there. If I had come there, a god, I also would have built.

How shall I tell what I saw? The towers are not all broken—here and there one still stands, like a great tree in a forest, and the birds nest high. But the towers themselves look blind, for the gods are gone. I saw a fish-hawk, catching fish in the river. I saw a little dance of white butterflies over a great heap of broken stones and columns. I went there and looked about me—there was a carved stone with cut-letters, broken in half. I can read letters but I could not understand these. They said UBTREAS. There was also the shattered image of a man or a god. It had been made of white stone and he wore his hair tied back like a woman's. His name was ASHING, as I read on the cracked half of a stone. I thought it wise to pray to ASHING, though I do not know that god.

How shall I tell what I saw? There was no smell of man left, on stone or metal. Nor were there many trees in that wilderness of stone. There are many pigeons, nesting and dropping in the towers—the gods must have loved them, or, perhaps, they used them for sacrifices. There are wild cats that roam the god-roads, green-eyed, unafraid of man. At night they wail like demons but they are not demons. The wild dogs are more dangerous, for they hunt in a pack, but them I did not meet till later. Everywhere there are the carved stones, carved with magical numbers or words.

I went north—I did not try to hide myself. When a god or a demon saw me, then I would die, but meanwhile I was no longer afraid. My hunger for knowledge burned in me—there was so much that I could not understand. After awhile, I knew that my belly was hungry. I could have hunted for my meat, but I did not hunt. It is known that the gods did not hunt as we do—they got their food from enchanted boxes and jars. Sometimes these are still found in the Dead Places—once, when I was a child and foolish, I opened such a jar and tasted it and found the food sweet. But my father found out and punished me for it strictly, for, often, that food is death. Now, though, I had long gone past what was forbidden, and I entered the likeliest towers, looking for the food of the gods.

I found it at last in the ruins of a great temple in the mid-city. A mighty temple it must have been, for the roof was painted like the sky at night with its stars—that much I could see, though the colors were faint and dim. It went down into great caves and tunnels—perhaps they kept their slaves there. But when I started to climb down, I heard the squeaking of rats, so I did not go—rats are unclean, and there must have been many tribes of them, from the squeaking. But near there, I found food, in the heart of a ruin, behind a door that still opened. I ate only the fruits from the jars —they had a very sweet taste. There was drink, too, in bottles of glass—the drink of the gods was strong and made my head swim. After I had eaten and drunk, I slept on the top of a stone, my bow at my side.

When I woke, the sun was low. Looking down from where I lay, I saw a dog sitting on his haunches. His tongue was hanging out of his mouth; he looked as if he were laughing. He was a big dog, with a gray-brown coat, as big as a wolf. I sprang up and shouted at him but he did not move—he just sat there as if he were laughing. I did not like that. When I reached for a stone to throw, he moved swiftly out of the way of the stone. He was not afraid of me; he looked at me as if I were meat. No doubt I could have killed him with an arrow, but I did not know if there were others. Moreover, night was falling.

I looked about me—not far away there was a great, broken god-road, leading north. The towers were high enough, but not so high, and while many of the dead houses were wrecked, there were some that stood. I went toward this god-road, keeping to the heights of the ruins, while the dog followed. When I had reached the god-road, I saw that there were others behind him. If I had slept later, they would have come upon me asleep and torn out my throat. As it was, they were sure enough of me; they did not hurry. When I went into the dead house, they kept watch at the entrance—doubtless they thought they would have a fine hunt. But a dog cannot open a door and I knew, from the books, that the gods did not like to live on the ground but on high.

I had just found a door I could open when the dogs decided to rush. Ha! They were surprised when I shut the door in their faces—it was a good door, of strong metal. I could hear their foolish baying beyond it but I did not stop to answer them. I was in darkness—I found stairs and climbed. There were many stairs, turning around till my head was dizzy. At the top was another door—I found the knob and opened it. I was in a long, small chamber—on one side of it was a bronze door that could not be opened, for it had no handle. Perhaps there was a magic word to open it but I did not have the word. I turned to the door in the opposite side of the wall. The lock of it was broken and I opened it and went in.

Within, there was a place of great riches. The god who lived there must have been a powerful god. The first room was a small anteroom—I waited there for some time, telling the spirits of the place that I came in peace and not as a robber. When it seemed to me that they had had time to hear me, I went on. Ah, what riches! Few, even, of the windows had been broken—it was all as it had been. The great windows that looked over the city had not been broken at all though they were dusty and streaked with many years. There were coverings on the floors, the colors not greatly faded, and the chairs were soft and deep. There were pictures upon the walls, very strange, very wonderful—I remember one of a bunch of flowers in a jar—if you came close to it, you could see nothing but bits of color, but if you stood away from it, the flowers might have been picked yesterday. It made my heart feel strange to look at this picture—and to look at the figure of a bird, in some hard clay, on a table and see it so like our birds. Everywhere there were books and writings, many in tongues that I could not read. The god who lived there must have been a wise god and full of knowledge. I felt I had right there, as I sought knowledge also.

Nevertheless, it was strange. There was a washing-place but no water—perhaps the gods washed in air. There was a cooking-place but no wood, and though there was a machine to cook food, there was no place to put fire in it. Nor were there candles or lamps—there were things that looked like lamps but they had neither oil nor wick. All these things were magic, but I touched them and lived—the magic had gone out of them. Let me tell one thing to show. In the washing-place, a thing said "Hot" but it was not hot to the touch—another thing said "Cold" but it was not cold. This must have been a strong magic but the magic was gone. I do not understand—they had ways—I wish that I knew.

It was close and dry and dusty in this house of the gods. I have said the magic was gone but that is not true—it had gone from the magic things but it had not gone from the place. I felt the spirits about me, weighing upon me. Nor had I ever slept in a Dead Place before—and yet, tonight, I must sleep there. When I thought of it, my tongue felt dry in my throat, in spite of my wish for knowledge. Almost I would have gone down again and faced the dogs, but I did not.

I had not gone through all the rooms when the darkness fell. When it fell, I went back to the big room looking over the city and made fire. There was a place to make fire and a box with wood in it, though I do not think they cooked there. I wrapped myself in a floor-covering and slept in front of the fire—I was very tired.

Now I tell what is very strong magic. I woke in the midst of the night. When I woke, the fire had gone out and I was cold. It seemed to me that all around me there were whisperings and voices. I closed my eyes to shut them out. Some will say that I slept again, but I do not think that I slept. I could feel the spirits drawing my spirit out of my body as a fish is drawn on a line.

Why should I lie about it? I am a priest and the son of a priest. If there are spirits, as they say, in the small Dead Places near us, what spirits must there not be in that great Place of the Gods? And would not they wish to speak? After such long years? I know that I felt myself drawn as a fish is drawn on a line. I had stepped out of my body—I could see my body asleep in front of the cold fire, but it was not I. I was drawn to look out upon the city of the gods.

It should have been dark, for it was night, but it was not dark. Everywhere there were lights—lines of light—circles and blurs of light —ten thousand torches would not have been the same. The sky itself was alight—you barely see the stars for the glow in the sky. I thought to myself "This is strong magic" and trembled. There was a roaring in my ears like the rushing of rivers. Then my eyes grew used to the light and my ears to the sound. I knew that I was seeing the city as it had been when the gods were alive.

That was a sight indeed—yes, that was a

sight: I could not have seen it in the body—my body would have died. Everywhere went the gods, on foot and in chariots—there were gods beyond number and counting and their chariots blocked the streets. They had turned night to day for their pleasure—they did not sleep with the sun. The noise of their coming and going was the noise of many waters. It was magic what they could do—it was magic what they did.

I looked out of another window—the great vines of their bridges were mended and the god-roads went east and west. Restless, restless, were the gods and always in motion! They burrowed tunnels under rivers—they flew in the air. With unbelievable tools they did giant works—no part of the earth was safe from them, for, if they wished for a thing, they summoned it from the other side of the world. And always, as they labored and rested, as they feasted and made love, there was a drum in their ears—the pulse of the giant city, beating and beating like a man's heart.

Were they happy? What is happiness to the gods? They were great, they were mighty, they were wonderful and terrible. As I looked upon them and their magic, I felt like a child—but a little more, it seemed to me, and they would pull down the moon from the sky. I saw them with wisdom beyond wisdom and knowledge beyond knowledge. And yet not all they did was well done—even I could see that—and yet their wisdom could not but grow until all was peace.

Then I saw their fate come upon them and that was terrible past speech. It came upon them as they walked the streets of their city. I have been in the fights with the Forest People —I have seen men die. But this was not like that. When gods war with gods, they use weapons we do not know. It was fire falling out of the sky and a mist that poisoned. It was the time of the Great Burning and the Destruction. They ran about like ants in the streets of their city—poor gods, poor gods! Then the towers began to fall. A few escaped—yes, a few. The legends tell it. But even after the city had become a Dead Place, for many years the poison was still in the ground. I saw it happen, I saw the last of them die. It was darkness over the broken city and I wept.

All this, I saw. I saw it as I have told it, though not in the body. When I woke in the morning, I was hungry, but I did not think first of my hunger for my heart was perplexed and confused. I knew the reason for the Dead Places but I did not see why it had happened. It seemed to me it should not have happened, with all the magic they had. I went through the house looking for an answer. There was so much in the house I could not understand—and yet I am a priest and the son of a priest. It was like being on one side of the great river, at night, with no light to show the way.

Then I saw the dead god. He was sitting in his chair, by the window, in a room I had not entered before and, for the first moment, I thought that he was alive. Then I saw the skin on the back of his hand—it was like dry leather. The room was shut, hot and dry—no doubt that had kept him as he was. At first I was afraid to approach him—then the fear left me. He was sitting looking out over the city—he was dressed in the clothes of the gods. His age was neither young nor old—I could not tell his age. But there was wisdom in his face and great sadness. I could see that he would have not run away. He had sat at his window, watching his city die—then he himself had died. But it is better to lose one's life than one's spirit—and you could see from the face that his spirit had not been lost. I knew that, if I touched him, he would fall into dust—and yet, there was something unconquered in the face.

That is all of my story, for then I knew he was a man—I knew then that they had been men, neither gods nor demons. It is a great knowledge, hard to tell and believe. They were men—they went a dark road, but they were men. I had no fear after that—I had no fear going home, though twice I fought off the dogs and once I was hunted for two days by the Forest People. When I saw my father again, I prayed and was purified. He touched my lips and my breast, he said, "You went away a boy. You come back a man and a priest." I said, "Father, they were men! I have been in the Place of the Gods and seen it! Now slay me, if it is the law—but still I know they were men."

He looked at me out of both eyes. He said, "The law is not always the same shape—you have done what you have done. I could not have done it in my time, but you come after me. Tell!"

I told and he listened. After that, I wished to tell all the people but he showed me otherwise. He said, "Truth is a hard deer to hunt. If you eat too much truth at once, you may die of the truth. It was not idly that our fathers forbade the Dead Places." He was right—it is better the truth should come little by little. I have learned that, being a priest. Perhaps, in the old days, they ate knowledge too fast.

Nevertheless, we make a beginning. It is not for the metal alone we go to the Dead Places now—there are the books and the writings.

They are hard to learn. And the magic tools are broken—but we can look at them and wonder. At least, we make a beginning. And, when I am chief priest we shall go beyond the great river. We shall go to the Place of the Gods—the place newyork—not one man but a company. We shall look for the images of the gods and find the god ASHING and the others—the gods Lincoln and Biltmore and Moses. But they were men who built the city, not gods or demons. They were men. I remember the dead man's face. They were men who were here before us. We must build again.

JOHNNY PYE
AND THE
FOOL-KILLER

✦

ILLUSTRATED BY *Charles Child*

I

YOU DON'T HEAR SO MUCH ABOUT THE FOOL-
killer these days, but when Johnny Pye was a
boy there was a good deal of talk about him.
Some said he was one kind of person, and some
said another, but most people agreed that he
came around fairly regular. Or, it seemed so to
Johnny Pye. But then, Johnny was an adopted
child, which is, maybe, why he took it so hard.

The miller and his wife had offered to raise

him, after his own folks died, and that was a good deed on their part. But, as soon as he lost his baby teeth and started acting the way most boys act, they started to come down on him like thunder, which wasn't so good. They were good people, according to their lights, but their lights were terrible strict ones, and they believed that the harder you were on a youngster, the better and brighter he got. Well, that may work with some children, but it didn't with Johnny Pye.

He was sharp enough and willing enough—as sharp and willing as most boys in Martinsville. But, somehow or other, he never seemed to be able to do the right things or say the right words—at least when he was home. Treat a boy like a fool and he'll act like a fool, I say, but there's some folks need convincing. The miller and his wife thought the way to smarten Johnny was to treat him like a fool, and finally they got so he pretty much believed it himself.

And that was hard on him, for he had a boy's imagination, and maybe a little more than most. He could stand the beatings and he did. But what he couldn't stand was the way things went at the mill. I don't suppose the miller intended to do it. But, as long as Johnny Pye could remember, whenever he heard of the death of somebody he didn't like, he'd say,

"Well, the Fool-Killer's come for so-and-so," and sort of smack his lips. It was, as you might say, a family joke, but the miller was a big man with a big red face, and it made a strong impression on Johnny Pye. Till, finally, he got a picture of the Fool-Killer, himself. He was a big man, too, in a checked shirt and corduroy trousers, and he went walking the ways of the world, with a hickory club that had a lump of lead in the end of it. I don't know how Johnny Pye got that picture so clear, but, to him, it was just as plain as the face of any human being in Martinsville. Now and then, just to test it, he'd ask a grown-up person, kind of timidly, if that was the way the Fool-Killer looked. And, of course, they'd generally laugh and tell him it was. Then Johnny would wake up at night, in his room over the mill, and listen for the Fool-Killer's step on the road and wonder when he was coming. But he was brave enough not to tell anybody that.

Finally, though, things got a little more than he could bear. He'd done some boy's trick or other—let the stones grind a little fine, maybe, when the miller wanted the meal ground coarse —just carelessness, you know. But he'd gotten two whippings for it, one from the miller and one from his wife, and at the end of it, the miller had said, "Well, Johnny Pye, the Fool-

Killer ought to be along for you most any day now. For I never did see a boy that was such a fool." Johnny looked to the miller's wife to see if she believed it, too, but she just shook her head and looked serious. So he went to bed that night, but he couldn't sleep, for every time a bough rustled or the mill wheel creaked, it seemed to him it must be the Fool-Killer. And, early next morning, before anybody was up, he packed such duds as he had in a bandanna handkerchief and ran away.

II

HE DIDN'T REALLY EXPECT TO GET AWAY FROM
the Fool-Killer very long—as far as he knew,
the Fool-Killer got you wherever you went. But
he thought he'd give him a run for his money,
at least. And when he got on the road, it was a
bright spring morning, and the first peace and
quiet he'd had in some time. So his spirits rose,
and he chunked a stone at a bullfrog as he went

along, just to show he was Johnny Pye and still doing business.

He hadn't gone more than three or four miles out of Martinsville, when he heard a buggy coming up the road behind him. He knew the Fool-Killer didn't need a buggy to catch you, so he wasn't afraid of it, but he stepped to the side of the road to let it pass. But it stopped, instead, and a black-whiskered man with a stovepipe hat looked out of it.

"Hello, bub," he said. "Is this the road for East Liberty?"

"My name's John Pye and I'm eleven years old," said Johnny, polite but firm, "and you take the next left fork for East Liberty. They say it's a pretty town—I've never been there myself." And he sighed a little, because he thought he'd like to see the world before the Fool-Killer caught up with him.

"H'm," said the man. "Stranger here too, eh? And what brings a smart boy like you on the road so early in the morning?"

"Oh," said Johnny Pye, quite honestly, "I'm running away from the Fool-Killer. For the miller says I'm a fool and his wife says I'm a fool and almost everybody in Martinsville says I'm a fool except little Susie Marsh. And the miller says the Fool-Killer's after me—so I thought I'd run away before he came."

The black-whiskered man sat in his buggy and wheezed for a while. When he got his breath back, "Well, jump in, bub," he said. "The miller may say you're a fool, but I think you're a right smart boy to be running away from the Fool-Killer all by yourself. And I don't hold with small-town prejudices and I need a right smart boy, so I'll give you a lift on the road."

"But, will I be safe from the Fool-Killer, if I'm with you?" said Johnny. "For, otherwise, it don't signify."

"Safe?" said the black-whiskered man, and wheezed again. "Oh, you'll be safe as houses. You see, I'm a herb doctor—and some folks think, a little in the Fool-Killer's line of business, myself. And I'll teach you a trade worth two of milling. So jump in, bub."

"Sounds all right the way you say it," said Johnny, "but my name's John Pye," and he jumped into the buggy. And they went rattling along toward East Liberty with the herb doctor talking and cutting jokes till Johnny thought he'd never met a pleasanter man. About half a mile from East Liberty, the doctor stopped at a spring.

"What are we stopping here for?" said Johnny Pye.

"Wait and see," said the doctor, and gave

him a wink. Then he got a haircloth trunk full of empty bottles out of the back of the buggy and made Johnny fill them with spring water and label them. Then he added a pinch of pink powder to each bottle and shook them up and corked them and stowed them away.

"What's that?" said Johnny, very interested.

"That's Old Doctor Waldo's Unparalleled Universal Remedy," said the doctor, reading from the label. "Made from the purest snake oil and secret Indian herbs, it cures rheumatism, blind staggers, headache, malaria, five kinds of fits, and spots in front of the eyes. It will also remove oil or grease stains, clean knives and silver, polish brass, and is strongly recommended as a general tonic and blood purifier. Small size, one dollar—family bottle, two dollars and a half."

"But I don't see any snake oil in it," said Johnny, puzzled, "or any secret Indian herbs."

"That's because you're not a fool," said the doctor, with another wink. "The Fool-Killer wouldn't, either. But most folks will."

And, that very same night, Johnny saw. For the doctor made his pitch in East Liberty and he did it handsome. He took a couple of flaring oil torches and stuck them on the sides of the buggy; he put on a diamond stickpin and did card tricks and told funny stories till he had the crowd goggle-eyed. As for Johnny, he let him play on the tambourine. Then he started talking about Doctor Waldo's Universal Remedy, and, with Johnny to help him, the bottles went like hot cakes. Johnny helped the doctor count the money afterward, and it was a pile.

"Well," said Johnny, "I never saw money made easier. You've got a fine trade, doctor."

"It's cleverness does it," said the doctor, and slapped him on the back. "Now a fool's content to stay in one place and do one thing, but the Fool-Killer never caught up with a good pitchman yet."

"Well, it's certainly lucky I met up with you," said Johnny, "and, if it's cleverness does it, I'll learn the trade or bust."

So he stayed with the doctor quite a while—in fact, till he could make up the remedy and do the card tricks almost as good as the doctor himself. And Johnny admired the doctor and the doctor liked Johnny, for Johnny was a biddable boy. But one night they came into a town where things didn't go as they usually did. The crowd gathered as usual, and the doctor did his tricks. But, all the time, Johnny could see a sharp-faced little fellow going through the crowd and whispering to one man and another. Till, at last, right in the middle of the doctor's spiel, the sharp-faced fellow gave a shout of "That's him all right! I'd know them whiskers anywhere!" and, with that, the crowd growled once and began to tear slats out of the nearest fence. Well, the next thing Johnny knew, he and the doctor were being ridden out of town on a rail, with the doctor's long coattails flying at every jounce.

They didn't hurt Johnny particular—him only being a boy. But they warned 'em both never to show their faces in that town again, and then they heaved the doctor into a thistle patch and went their ways.

"Owoo!" said the doctor, "ouch!" as Johnny was helping him out of the thistle patch. "Go easy with those thistles! And why didn't you give me the office, you blame little fool?"

"Office?" said Johnny. "What office?"

"When that sharp-nosed man started snooping around," said the doctor. "I thought that infernal main street looked familiar—I was through there two years ago, selling solid gold watches for a dollar apiece."

"But the works to a solid gold watch would be worth more than that," said Johnny.

"There weren't any works," said the doctor, with a groan, "but there was a nice lively beetle inside each case and it made the prettiest tick you ever heard."

"Well, that certainly was a clever idea," said Johnny. "I'd never have thought of that."

"Clever?" said the doctor. "Ouch—it was ruination! But who'd have thought the fools would bear a grudge for two years? And now we've lost the horse and buggy, too—not to speak of the bottles and the money. Well, there's lots more tricks to be played and we'll start again."

But, though he liked the doctor, Johnny began to feel dubious. For it occurred to him that, if all the doctor's cleverness got him was being ridden out of town on a rail, he couldn't be so far away from the Fool-Killer as he thought. And, sure enough, as he was going to sleep that night, he seemed to hear the Fool-Killer's footsteps coming after him—step, step, step. He pulled his jacket up over his ears, but he couldn't shut it out. So, when the doctor had got in the way of starting business over again, he and Johnny parted company. The doctor didn't bear any grudge; he shook hands with Johnny and told him to remember that cleverness was power. And Johnny went on with his running away.

III

HE GOT TO A TOWN AND THERE WAS A STORE WITH a sign in the window, BOY WANTED, so he went in. There, sure enough, was the merchant, sitting at his desk, and a fine, important man he looked, in his black broadcloth suit.

Johnny tried to tell him about the Fool-Killer, but the merchant wasn't interested in that. He just looked Johnny over and saw that he looked biddable and strong for his age. "But, remem-

84

ber, no fooling around, boy!" said the merchant sternly, after he'd hired him.

"No fooling around?" said Johnny, with the light of hope in his eyes.

"No," said the merchant, meaningly. "We've no room for fools in this business, I can tell you! You work hard, and you'll rise. But, if you've got any foolish notions, just knock them on the head and forget them."

Well, Johnny was glad enough to promise that, and he stayed with the merchant a year and a half. He swept out the store, and he put the shutters up and took them down; he ran errands and wrapped up packages and learned to keep busy twelve hours a day. And, being a biddable boy and an honest one, he rose, just like the merchant had said. The merchant raised his wages and let him begin to wait on customers and learn accounts. And then, one night, Johnny woke up in the middle of the night. And it seemed to him he heard, far away but getting nearer, the steps of the Fool-Killer after him—tramping, tramping, tramping.

He went to the merchant next day and said, "Sir, I'm sorry to tell you this, but I'll have to be moving on."

"Well, I'm sorry to hear that, Johnny," said the merchant, "for you've been a good boy. And, if it's a question of salary—"

"It isn't that," said Johnny, "but tell me one thing, sir, if you don't mind my asking. Supposing I did stay with you—where would I end?"

The merchant smiled. "That's a hard question to answer," he said, "and I'm not much given to compliments. But I started, myself, as a boy, sweeping out the store. And you're a bright youngster with lots of go-ahead. I don't see why, if you stuck to it, you shouldn't make the same kind of success that I have."

"And what's that?" said Johnny.

The merchant began to look irritated, but he kept his smile.

"Well," he said, "I'm not a boastful man, but I'll tell you this. Ten years ago I was the richest man in town. Five years ago, I was the richest man in the county. And five years from now—well, I aim to be the richest man in the state."

His eyes kind of glittered as he said it, but Johnny was looking at his face. It was sallow-skinned and pouchy, with the jaw as hard as a rock. And it came upon Johnny that moment that, though he'd known the merchant a year and a half, he'd never really seen him enjoy himself except when he was driving a bargain.

"Sorry, sir," he said, "but, if it's like that, I'll certainly have to go. Because, you see, I'm running away from the Fool-Killer, and, if I stayed here and got to be like you, he'd certainly catch up with me in no—"

"Why, you impertinent young cub!" roared the merchant, with his face gone red all of a sudden. "Get your money from the cashier!" and Johnny was on the road again before you could say "Jack Robinson." But, this time, he was used to it, and walked off whistling.

Well, after that, he hired out to quite a few different people, but I won't go into all of his adventures. He worked for an inventor for a while, and they split up because Johnny happened to ask him what would be the good of his patent, self-winding, perpetual-motion machine, once he did get it invented. And, while the inventor talked big about improving the human race and the beauties of science, it was plain he didn't know. So that night, Johnny heard the steps of the Fool-Killer, far off but coming closer, and, next morning, he went away. Then he stayed with a minister for a while, and he certainly hated to leave him, for the minister was a good man. But they got talking one evening and, as it chanced, Johnny asked him what happened to people who didn't believe in his particular religion. Well, the minister was broad-minded, but there's only one answer to that. He admitted they might be good folks—he even admitted they mightn't exactly go to hell—but he couldn't let them into heaven, no, not the best and the wisest of them, for there were the specifications laid down by creed and church, and, if you didn't fulfill them, you didn't.

So Johnny had to leave him, and, after that, he went with an old drunken fiddler for a while. He wasn't a good man, I guess, but he could play till the tears ran down your cheeks. And, when he was playing his best, it seemed to Johnny that the Fool-Killer was very far away. For, in spite of his faults and his weaknesses, while he played, there was might in the man. But he died drunk in a ditch, one night, with Johnny to hold his head, and, while he left Johnny his fiddle, it didn't do Johnny much good. For, while Johnny could play a tune, he couldn't play like the fiddler—it wasn't in his fingers.

Then it chanced that Johnny took up with a company of soldiers. He was still too young to enlist, but they made a kind of pet of him, and everything went swimmingly for a while. For the captain was the bravest man Johnny had ever seen, and he had an answer for everything, out of regulations and the Articles of War. But then they went West to fight Indians and the same old trouble cropped up again. For, one night the captain said to him, "Johnny, we're going to fight the enemy tomorrow, but you'll stay in camp."

"Oh, I don't want to do that," said Johnny; "I want to be in on the fighting."

"It's an order," said the captain, grimly. Then he gave Johnny certain instructions and a letter to take to his wife.

"For the colonel's a copper-plated fool," he said, "and we're walking straight into an ambush."

"Why don't you tell him that?" said Johnny.

"I have," said the captain, "but he's the colonel."

"Colonel or no colonel," said Johnny, "if he's a fool, somebody ought to stop him."

"You can't do that, in an army," said the captain. "Orders are orders." But it turned out the captain was wrong about it, for, next day, before they could get moving, the Indians attacked, and got badly licked. When it was all over, "Well, it was a good fight," said the captain, professionally. "All the same, if they'd waited and laid an ambush, they'd have had our hair. But, as it was, they didn't stand a chance."

"But why didn't they lay an ambush?" said Johnny.

"Well," said the captain, "I guess they had

their orders too. And now, how would you like to be a soldier?"

"Well, it's a nice outdoors life, but I'd like to think it over," said Johnny. For he knew the captain was brave and he knew the Indians had been brave—you couldn't find two braver sets of people. But, all the same, when he thought the whole thing over, he seemed to hear steps in the sky. So he soldiered to the end of the campaign and then he left the Army, though the captain told him he was making a mistake.

By now, of course, he wasn't a boy any longer; he was getting to be a young man with a young man's thoughts and feelings. And, half the time, nowadays, he'd forget about the Fool-Killer except as a dream he'd had when he was a boy. He could even laugh at it now and then, and think what a fool he'd been to believe there was such a man.

But, all the same, the desire in him wasn't satisfied, and something kept driving him on. He'd have called it ambitiousness, now, but it came to the same thing. And with every new trade he tried, sooner or later would come the dream—the dream of the big man in the checked shirt and corduroy pants, walking the ways of the world with his hickory stick in one hand. It made him angry to have that dream, now, but it had a singular power over him. Till, finally, when he was turned twenty or so, he got scared.

"Fool-Killer or no Fool-Killer," he said to himself, "I've got to ravel this matter out. For there must be some one thing a man could tie to, and be sure he wasn't a fool. I've tried cleverness and money and half a dozen other things, and they don't seem to be the answer. So now I'll try book learning and see what comes of that."

So he read all the books he could find, and whenever he'd seem to hear the steps of the Fool-Killer coming for the authors—and that was frequent—he'd try and shut his ears. But some books said one thing was best and some another, and he couldn't rightly decide.

"Well," he said to himself, when he'd read and read till his head felt as stuffed with book learning as a sausage with meat, "it's interesting, but it isn't exactly contemporaneous. So I think I'll go down to Washington and ask the wise men there. For it must take a lot of wisdom to run a country like the United States, and if there's people who can answer my questions, it's there they ought to be found."

IV

SO HE PACKED HIS BAG AND OFF TO WASHINGTON he went. He was modest, for a youngster, and he didn't intend to try and see the President right away. He thought probably a congressman was about his size. So he saw a congressman, and the congressman told him the thing to be was an upstanding young American and vote the Republican ticket—which sounded all right to Johnny Pye, but not exactly what he was after.

Then he went to a senator, and the senator told him to be an upstanding young American and vote the Democratic ticket—which sounded all right, too, but not what he was after, either. And, somehow, though both men had been impressive and affable, right in the middle of their speeches he'd seemed to hear steps—you know.

But a man has to eat, whatever else he does, and Johnny found he'd better buckle down and get himself a job. It happened to be with the first congressman he struck, for that one came from Martinsville, which is why Johnny went to him in the first place. And, in a little while, he forgot his search entirely and the Fool-Killer, too, for the congressman's niece came East to visit him, and she was the Susie Marsh that Johnny had sat next in school. She'd been pretty then, but she was prettier now, and as soon as Johnny Pye saw her, his heart gave a jump and a thump.

"And don't think we don't remember you in Martinsville, Johnny Pye," she said, when her uncle had explained who his new clerk was. "Why, the whole town'll be excited when I write home. We've heard all about your killing Indians and inventing perpetual motion and traveling around the country with a famous doctor and making a fortune in dry goods and —oh, it's a wonderful story!"

"Well," said Johnny, and coughed, "some of that's just a little bit exaggerated. But it's nice of you to be interested. So they don't think I'm a fool any more, in Martinsville?"

"I never thought you were a fool," said Susie with a little smile, and Johnny felt his heart give another bump.

"And I always knew you were pretty, but never how pretty till now," said Johnny, and coughed again. "But, speaking of old times, how's the miller and his wife? For I did leave them right sudden, and while there were faults on both sides, I must have been a trial to them too."

"They've gone the way of all flesh," said Susie Marsh, "and there's a new miller now. But he isn't very well-liked, to tell the truth, and he's letting the mill run down."

"That's a pity," said Johnny, "for it was a likely mill." Then he began to ask her more questions and she began to remember things too. Well, you know how the time can go when two youngsters get talking like that.

Johnny Pye never worked so hard in his life as he did that winter. And it wasn't the Fool-Killer he thought about—it was Susie Marsh. First he thought she loved him and then he was sure she didn't, and then he was betwixt and between, and all perplexed and confused. But, finally, it turned out all right and he had her promise, and Johnny Pye knew he was the happiest man in the world. And that night, he waked up in the night and heard the Fool-Killer coming after him—step, step, step.

He didn't sleep much after that, and he came down to breakfast hollow-eyed. But his uncle-to-be didn't notice that—he was rubbing his hands and smiling.

"Put on your best necktie, Johnny!" he said, very cheerful, "for I've got an appointment with the President today, and, just to show I approve of my niece's fiancé, I'm taking you along."

"The President!" said Johnny, all dumbfounded.

"Yes," said Congressman Marsh, "you see, there's a little bill—well, we needn't go into that. But slick down your back hair, Johnny—we'll make Martinsville proud of us this day!"

Then a weight seemed to go from Johnny's shoulders and a load from his heart. He wrung Mr. Marsh's hand.

"Thank you, Uncle Eben!" he said. "I can't thank you enough." For, at last, he knew he was going to look upon a man that was bound to be safe from the Fool-Killer—and it seemed to him if he could just once do that, all his troubles and searchings would be ended.

Well, it doesn't signify which President it was—you can take it from me that he was President and a fine-looking man. He'd just been elected, too, so he was lively as a trout, and the saddle galls he'd get from Congress hadn't even begun to show. Anyhow, there he was, and Johnny feasted his eyes on him. For if there was anybody in the country the Fool-Killer couldn't bother, it must be a man like this.

The President and the congressman talked politics for a while, and then it was Johnny's turn.

"Well, young man," said the President, affably, "and what can I do for you—for you look to me like a fine, upstanding young American."

The congressman cut in quick before Johnny could open his mouth.

"Just a word of advice, Mr. President," he said. "Just a word in season. For my young friend's led an adventurous life, but now he's going to marry my niece and settle down. And what he needs most of all is a word of ripe wisdom from you."

"Well," said the President, looking at Johnny rather keenly, "if that's all he needs, a short horse is soon curried. I wish most of my callers wanted as little."

But, all the same, he drew Johnny out, as such men can, and before Johnny knew it, he was telling his life story.

"Well," said the President, at the end, "you certainly have been a rolling stone, young man. But there's nothing wrong in that. And, for one of your varied experience there's one obvious career. Politics!" he said, and slapped his fist in his hand.

"Well," said Johnny, scratching his head, "of course, since I've been in Washington, I've thought of that. But I don't know that I'm rightly fitted."

"You can write a speech," said Congressman Marsh, quite thoughtful, "for you've helped me with mine. You're a likable fellow too. And you were born poor and worked up—and you've even got a war-record—why, hell! Excuse me, Mr. President!—he's worth five hundred votes just as he stands!"

"I—I'm more than honored by you two gentlemen," said Johnny, abashed and flattered, "but supposing I did go into politics—where would I end up?"

The President looked sort of modest.

"The Presidency of the United States," said he, "is within the legitimate ambition of every

American citizen. Provided he can get elected, of course."

"Oh," said Johnny, feeling dazzled, "I never thought of that. Well, that's a great thing. But it must be a great responsibility too."

"It is," said the President, looking just like his pictures on the campaign buttons.

"Why, it must be an awful responsibility!" said Johnny. "I can't hardly see how a mortal man can bear it. Tell me, Mr. President," he said, "may I ask you a question?"

"Certainly," said the President, looking prouder and more responsible and more and more like his picture on the campaign buttons every minute.

"Well," said Johnny, "it sounds like a fool question, but it's this: This is a great big country of ours, Mr. President, and it's got the most amazing lot of different people in it. How can any President satisfy all those people at one time? Can you yourself, Mr. President?"

The President looked a bit taken aback for a minute. But then he gave Johnny Pye a statesman's glance.

"With the help of God," he said, solemnly, "and in accordance with the principles of our great party, I intend—"

But Johnny didn't even hear the end of the sentence. For, even as the President was speaking, he heard a step outside in the corridor and he knew, somehow, it wasn't the step of a secretary or a guard. He was glad the President had said "with the help of God" for that sort of softened the step. And when the President finished, Johnny bowed.

"Thank you, Mr. President," he said; "that's what I wanted to know. And now I'll go back to Martinsville, I guess."

"Go back to Martinsville?" said the President, surprised.

"Yes, sir," said Johnny. "For I don't think I'm cut out for politics."

"And is that all you have to say to the President of the United States?" said his uncle-to-be, in a fume.

But the President had been thinking, meanwhile, and he was a bigger man than the congressman.

"Wait a minute, congressman," he said. "This young man's honest, at least, and I like his looks. Moreover, of all the people who've come to see me in the last six months, he's the only one who hasn't wanted something—except the White House cat, and I guess she wanted something, too, because she meowed. You don't want to be President, young man—and, confidentially, I don't blame you. But how would you like to be postmaster at Martinsville?"

"Postmaster at Martinsville?" said Johnny. "But—"

"Oh, it's only a tenth-class post office," said the President, "but, for once in my life, I'll do something because I want to, and let Congress yell its head off. Come—is it yes or no?"

Johnny thought of all the places he'd been and all the trades he'd worked at. He thought, queerly enough, of the old drunk fiddler dead in the ditch, but he knew he couldn't be that. Mostly, though, he thought of Martinsville and Susie Marsh. And, though he'd just heard the Fool-Killer's step, he defied the Fool-Killer.

"Why, it's yes, of course, Mr. President," he said, "for then I can marry Susie."

"That's as good a reason as you'll find," said the President. "And now, I'll just write a note."

V

WELL, HE WAS AS GOOD AS HIS WORD, AND JOHNNY
and his Susie were married and went back to
live in Martinsville. And, as soon as Johnny
learned the ways of postmastering, he found it
as good a trade as most. There wasn't much
mail in Martinsville, but, in between whiles, he
ran the mill, and that was a good trade too. And
all the time, he knew, at the back of his mind,
that he hadn't quite settled accounts with the
Fool-Killer. But he didn't much care about
that, for he and Susie were happy. And after a

while they had a child, and that was the most remarkable experience that had ever happened to any young couple, though the doctor said it was a perfectly normal baby.

One evening, when his son was about a year old, Johnny Pye took the river road, going home. It was a mite longer than the hill road, but it was the cool of the evening, and there's times when a man likes to walk by himself, fond as he may be of his wife and family.

He was thinking of the way things had turned out for him, and they seemed to him pretty astonishing and singular, as they do to most folks, when you think them over. In fact, he was thinking so hard that, before he knew it, he'd almost stumbled over an old scissors grinder who'd set up his grindstone and tools by the side of the road. The scissors grinder had his cart with him, but he'd turned the horse out to graze—and a lank, old, white horse it was, with every rib showing. And he was very busy, putting an edge on a scythe.

"Oh, sorry," said Johnny Pye. "I didn't know anybody was camping here. But you might come round to my house tomorrow—my wife's got some knives that need sharpening." Then he stopped, for the old man gave him a long, keen look.

"Why, it's you, Johnny Pye," said the old

man. "And how do you do, Johnny Pye! You've been a long time coming—in fact, now and then, I thought I'd have to fetch you. But you're here at last."

Johnny Pye was a grown man now, but he began to tremble.

"But it isn't you!" he said, wildly. "I mean you're not him! Why, I've known how he looks all my life! He's a big man, with a checked shirt, and he carries a hickory stick with a lump of lead in one end."

"Oh, no," said the scissors grinder, quite quiet. "You may have thought of me that way, but that's not the way I am." And Johnny Pye heard the scythe go whet-whet-whet on the stone. The old man ran some water on it and looked at the edge. Then he shook his head as if the edge didn't quite satisfy him. "Well, Johnny, are you ready?" he said, after a while.

"Ready?" said Johnny, in a hoarse voice. "Of course I'm not ready."

"That's what they all say," said the old man, nodding his head, and the scythe went whet-whet on the stone.

Johnny wiped his brow and started to argue it out.

"You see, if you'd found me earlier," he said, "or later. I don't want to be unreasonable, but I've got a wife and a child."

"Most has wives and many has children," said the old man, grimly, and the scythe went whet-whet on the stone as he pushed the treadle. And a shower of sparks flew, very clear and bright, for the night had begun to fall.

"Oh, stop that damn racket and let a man think for a minute!" said Johnny, desperate. "I can't go, I tell you. I won't. It isn't time. It's—"

The old man stopped the grindstone and pointed with the scythe at Johnny Pye.

"Tell me one good reason," he said. "There's men would be missed in the world, but are you one of them? A clever man might be missed, but are you a clever man?"

"No," said Johnny, thinking of the herb doctor. "I had a chance to be clever, but I gave it up."

"One," said the old man, ticking off on his fingers. "Well, a rich man might be missed—by some. But you aren't rich, I take it."

"No," said Johnny, thinking of the merchant, "nor wanted to be."

"Two," said the old man. "Cleverness—riches —they're done. But there's still martial bravery and being a hero. There might be an argument to make, if you were one of those."

Johnny Pye shuddered a little, remembering the way that battlefield had looked, out West, when the Indians were dead and the fight over.

107

"No," he said, "I've fought, but I'm not a hero."

"Well, then, there's religion," said the old man, sort of patient, "and science, and—but what's the use? We know what you did with those. I might feel a trifle of compunction if I had to deal with a President of the United States. But—"

"Oh, you know well enough I ain't President," said Johnny, with a groan. "Can't you get it over with and be done?"

"You're not putting up a very good case," said the old man, shaking his head. "I'm surprised at you, Johnny. Here you spend your youth running away from being a fool. And yet, what's the first thing you do, when you're man grown? Why, you marry a girl, settle down in your home town, and start raising children when you don't know how they'll turn out. You might have known I'd catch up with you, then —you just put yourself in my way."

"Fool I may be," said Johnny Pye in his agony, "and if you take it like that, I guess we're all fools. But Susie's my wife, and my child's my child. And, as for work in the world —well, somebody has to be postmaster, or folks wouldn't get the mail."

"Would it matter much if they didn't?" said the old man, pointing his scythe.

"Well, no, I don't suppose it would, considering what's on the post cards," said Johnny Pye. "But while it's my business to sort it, I'll sort it as well as I can."

The old man whetted his scythe so hard that a long shower of sparks flew out on the grass.

"Well," he said, "I've got my job, too, and I do it likewise. But I'll tell you what I'll do. You're coming my way, no doubt of it, but, looking you over, you don't look quite ripe yet. So I'll let you off for a while. For that matter," said he, "if you'll answer one question of mine —how a man can be a human being and not be a fool —I'll let you off permanent. It'll be the first time in history," he said, "but you've got to do something on your own hook, once in a while. And now you can walk along, Johnny Pye."

With that he ground the scythe till the sparks flew out like the tail of a comet and Johnny Pye walked along. The air of the meadow had never seemed so sweet to him before.

All the same, even with his relief, he didn't quite forget, and sometimes Susie had to tell the children not to disturb father because he was thinking. But time went ahead, as it does, and pretty soon Johnny Pye found he was forty. He'd never expected to be forty, when he was young, and it kind of surprised him. But there

it was, though he couldn't say he felt much
different, except now and then when he stooped
over. And he was a solid citizen of the town,
well-liked and well-respected, with a growing
family and a stake in the community, and when
he thought those things over, they kind of surprised him too. But, pretty soon, it was as if
things had always been that way.

It was after his eldest son had been drowned
out fishing that Johnny Pye met the scissors
grinder again. But this time, he was bitter and
distracted, and, if he could have got to the old
man, he'd have done him a mortal harm. But,
somehow or other, when he tried to come to
grips with him, it was like reaching for air and
mist. He could see the sparks fly from the
ground scythe, but he couldn't even touch the
wheel.

"You coward!" said Johnny Pye. "Stand up
and fight like a man!" But the old man just
nodded his head and the wheel kept grinding
and grinding.

"Why couldn't you have taken me?" said
Johnny Pye, as if those words had never been
said before. "What's the sense in all this? Why
can't you take me now?"

Then he tried to wrench the scythe from the
old man's hands, but he couldn't touch it. And

then he fell down and lay on the grass for a while.

"Time passes," said the old man, nodding his head. "Time passes."

"It will never cure the grief I have for my son," said Johnny Pye.

"It will not," said the old man, nodding his head. "But time passes. Would you leave your wife a widow and your other children fatherless for the sake of your grief?"

"No, God help me!" said Johnny Pye. "That wouldn't be right for a man."

"Then go home to your house, Johnny Pye," said the old man. And Johnny Pye went, but there were lines in his face that hadn't been there before.

VI

AND TIME PASSED, LIKE THE FLOW OF THE RIVER, and Johnny Pye's children married and had houses and children of their own. And Susie's hair grew white, and her back grew bent, and when Johnny Pye and his children followed her to her grave, folks said she'd died in the fullness of years, but that was hard for Johnny Pye to believe. Only folks didn't talk as plain as they used to, and the sun didn't heat as much, and sometimes, before dinner, he'd go to sleep in his chair.

114

And once, after Susie had died, the President of those days came through Martinsville and Johnny Pye shook hands with him and there was a piece in the paper about his shaking hands with two Presidents, fifty years apart. Johnny Pye cut out the clipping and kept it in his pocketbook. He liked this President all right, but, as he told people, he wasn't a patch on the other one fifty years ago. Well, you couldn't expect it—you didn't have Presidents these days, not to call them Presidents. All the same, he took a lot of satisfaction in the clipping.

He didn't get down to the river road much any more—it wasn't too long a walk, of course, but he just didn't often feel like it. But, one day, he slipped away from the granddaughter that was taking care of him, and went. It was kind of a steep road, really—he didn't remember its being so steep.

"Well," said the scissors grinder, "and good afternoon to you, Johnny Pye."

"You'll have to talk a little louder," said Johnny Pye. "My hearing's perfect, but folks don't speak as plain as they used to. Stranger in town?"

"Oh, so that's the way it is," said the scissors grinder.

"Yes, that's the way it is," said Johnny Pye. He knew he ought to be afraid of this fellow, now he'd put on his spectacles and got a good look at him, but for the life of him, he couldn't remember why.

"I know just who you are," he said, a little fretfully. "Never forgot a face in my life, and your name's right on the tip of my tongue—"

"Oh, don't bother about names," said the scissors grinder. "We're old acquaintances. And I asked you a question, years ago—do you remember that?"

"Yes," said Johnny Pye, "I remember." Then he began to laugh—a high, old man's laugh. "And of all the fool questions I ever was asked," he said, "that certainly took the cake."

"Oh?" said the scissors grinder.

"Uh-huh," said Johnny Pye. "For you asked me how a man could be a human being and yet not be a fool. And the answer is—when he's dead and gone and buried. Any fool would know that."

"That so?" said the scissors grinder.

"Of course," said Johnny Pye. "I ought to know. I'll be ninety-two next November, and I've shook hands with two Presidents. The first President I shook—"

"I'll be interested to hear about that," said the scissors grinder, "but we've got a little business, first. For, if all human beings are fools, how does the world get ahead?"

116

"Oh, there's lots of other things," said Johnny Pye, kind of impatient. "There's the brave and the wise and the clever—and they're apt to roll it ahead as much as an inch. But it's all mixed in together. For, Lord, it's only some fool kind of creature that would have crawled out of the sea to dry land in the first place—or got dropped from the Garden of Eden, if you like it better that way. You can't depend on the kind of folks people think they are—you've got to go by what they do. And I wouldn't give much for a man that some folks hadn't thought was a fool, in his time."

"Well," said the scissors grinder, "you've answered my question—at least as well as you could, which is all you can expect of a man. So I'll keep my part of the bargain."

"And what was that?" said Johnny. "For, while it's all straight in my head, I don't quite recollect the details."

"Why," said the scissors grinder, rather testy, "I'm to let you go, you old fool! You'll never see me again till the Last Judgment. There'll be trouble in the office about it," said he, "but you've got to do what you like, once in a while."

"Phew!" said Johnny Pye. "That needs thinking over!" And he scratched his head.

"Why?" said the scissors grinder, a bit affronted. "It ain't often I offer a man eternal life."

"Well," said Johnny Pye, "I take it very kind, but, you see, it's this way." He thought for a moment. "No," he said, "you wouldn't understand. You can't have touched seventy yet, by your looks, and no young man would."

"Try me," said the scissors grinder.

"Well," said Johnny Pye, "it's this way," and he scratched his head again. "I'm not saying— if you'd made the offer forty years ago, or even twenty. But, well, now, let's just take one detail. Let's say teeth."

"Well, of course," said the scissors grinder, "naturally—I mean you could hardly expect me to do anything about that."

"I thought so," said Johnny Pye. "Well, you see, these are good, bought teeth, but I'm sort of tired of hearing them click. And spectacles, I suppose, the same?"

"I'm afraid so," said the scissors grinder. "I can't interfere with time, you know—that's not my department. And, frankly, you couldn't expect, at a hundred and eighty, let's say, to be quite the man you was at ninety. But still, you'd be a wonder!"

"Maybe so," said Johnny Pye, "but, you see —well, the truth is, I'm an old man now. You wouldn't think it to look at me, but it's so. And my friends—well, they're gone—and Susie and the boy—and somehow you don't get as close to the younger people, except the children. And to keep on just going and going till Judgment Day, with nobody around to talk to that had real horse sense—well, no, sir, it's a handsome offer but I just don't feel up to accepting it. It may not be patriotic of me, and I feel sorry for Martinsville. It'd do wonders for the climate and the chamber of commerce to have a leading citizen live till Judgment Day. But a man's got to do as he likes, at least once in his life." He stopped and looked at the scissors grinder. "I'll admit, I'd kind of like to beat out Ike Leavis," he said. "To hear him talk, you'd think nobody had ever pushed ninety before. But I suppose—"

"I'm afraid we can't issue a limited policy," said the scissors grinder.

"Well," said Johnny Pye, "I just thought of it. And Ike's all right." He waited a moment. "Tell me," he said, in a low voice. "Well, you know what I mean. Afterwards. I mean, if you're likely to see"—he coughed—"your friends again. I mean, if it's so."

"I can't tell you that," said the scissors grinder. "I only go so far."

"Well, there's no harm in asking," said Johnny Pye, rather humbly. He peered into the darkness; a last shower of sparks flew from the scythe, then the whir of the wheel stopped.

"H'm," said Johnny Pye, testing the edge. "That's a well-ground scythe. But they used to grind 'em better in the old days." He listened and looked, for a moment, anxiously. "Oh, Lordy!" he said, "there's Helen coming to look for me. She'll take me back to the house."

"Not this time," said the scissors grinder. "Yes, there isn't bad steel in that scythe. Well, let's go, Johnny Pye."

ABOUT THE AUTHOR

Stephen Vincent Benét received his B.A. and M.A. from Yale University, where he served as editor of *The Yale Literary Magazine* and numbered among his friends Thornton Wilder, Archibald MacLeish, and Philip Barry. Later Mr. Benét went to France for two years on a Guggenheim Fellowship and produced his classic American epic poem of the Civil War, JOHN BROWN'S BODY, which was awarded the Pulitzer Prize for poetry in 1929. He has also written dramatic monologues, radio scripts, novels, and collections of poems and short stories. WESTERN STAR, an unfinished narrative on American history, was published posthumously and won the Pulitzer Prize in 1943. THE DEVIL AND DANIEL WEBSTER originally appeared in a collection, THIRTEEN O'CLOCK, and has been translated into many different media: first a play, then a musical, and finally a motion picture.

POCKET BOOKS

ARCHWAY
PAPERBACKS

Other titles you will enjoy

29840 STAR KA'AT, by Andre Norton and Dorothy Madlee. Illustrated by Bernard Colonna. An exciting rescue mission from outer space opens the way for a special friendship between two super-cats and two courageous kids. ($1.25)

29817 FOG MAGIC, by Julia L. Sauer. Illustrated by Lynd Ward. When Greta walks through the fog, she starts off on an adventure that takes her back to the past of one hundred years ago. ($1.25)

29730 THE CITY UNDER GROUND, by Suzanne Martel. Illustrated by Don Sibley. Centuries after a nuclear holocaust, a boy who lives in a surviving underground city dares to explore the outside world. (95¢)

29873 THE GHOSTS, by Antonia Barber. The ghosts of two children who died a century ago call on Lucy and Jamie to go back in time and try to change the events that led up to their murder. ($1.50)

(If your bookseller does not have the titles you want, you may order them by sending the retail price, plus 50¢ for postage and handling, to: Mail Service Department, POCKET BOOKS, a Simon & Schuster Division of Gulf & Western Corporation, 1230 Avenue of the Americas, New York, N. Y. 10020. Please enclose check or money order—do not send cash.)

29943